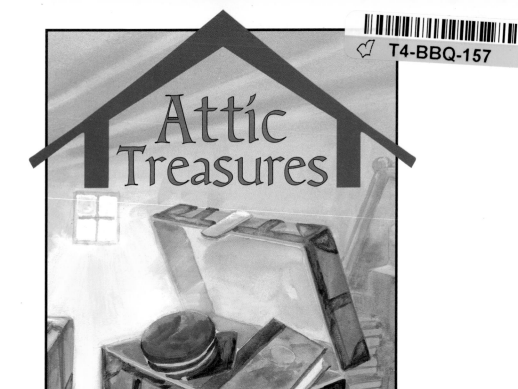

Attic Treasures

by Barbara Lawson • illustrated by Sue Rother

SCHOLASTIC INC.

New York   Toronto   London   Auckland   Sydney
Mexico City   New Delhi   Hong Kong   Buenos Aires

Developed by Kirchoff/Wohlberg, Inc., in cooperation with Scholastic Inc.

Glen and Flora stood in the dust of their grandparents' attic. All around them were boxes, trunks, and old clothes.

"I don't see any games or toys," said Glen. "Grandmother said we might find something fun up here."

"I hope we do," said Flora. "I'm tired of TV and it's too rainy to go outside and play."

Glen opened an old cardboard box. "Help me look, Flora. Who knows what we'll find? There could be all sorts of surprises!"

In the cardboard box were some rusty hammers, screwdrivers, bolts, and nails. "Want to build something?" asked Glen with a smile.

Flora knew not to touch them. "They look too old for that," she said. She dug through a crate by the chimney. "Here are some old dishes! They're really pretty. We could have a tea party."

Glen rolled his eyes. "No, thanks."

The two children looked through more boxes, finding only magazines, books, a carved duck, and some moth-eaten clothes.

A few minutes later, Flora discovered an old trunk. It was hidden beneath a layer of old blankets and dust.

"Look!" she said. "I wonder what this is. It has a lock on it! It must be a secret!"

"I wish we could open it," said Glen. "We have no key."

Flora looked around. She saw something shiny on the sill of the attic window. "I think that's a key!" she said. She had to duck beneath a low ceiling beam so she wouldn't bump her head. She grabbed the piece of metal. "It is a key! Let's try it!"

Flora sat down beside Glen. "I hope it works," she said. "I know there are wonderful things inside. Why else would it be locked?"

Slowly, she slid the tip of the key into the lock. With a click, the lock popped open.

Glen cheered. Flora pushed the lid up. Bits of dust flew into the air like gnats.

The children looked inside. Their smiles faded at once.

"More books," said Glen. "And some clothes. I thought there would be games or some treasure."

Flora dug inside the trunk. "Maybe there's gold at the bottom," she said.

They wiggled their fingers deep into the trunk, under books, papers, and old clothes. But there was no gold at all.

Glen and Flora sat back on their heels. Their noses were covered with dust.

Glen sneezed. Then he said, "Let's close it. This trunk is a waste of time."

"Wait," said Flora. She pulled an old red, leather-covered book from the trunk. "Look."

"It's just another book," said Glen.

"I don't think so," said Flora. She rubbed the dirt from the cover. "It says, 'Log of Salty Jones, Captain of the *Sea Skipper.*'"

"Salty Jones," said Glen. "He was our great-great-grandfather!"

"That's right," said Flora. "But nobody knows much about him. He was a sea captain, and here is his journal."

Glen wrapped his arms around his knees. "I wonder if he had any adventures?" he asked. "Let's read and find out."

Flora carefully opened to the first page and read out loud.

May 12. All through the night I heard the wind blow as loud as a lion's roar. I was afraid the Sea Skipper might tip over, but she held on. Above my bunk, the lantern swayed back and forth. Shadows ran around the floor like a cat after mice.

I went topside at midnight to check on my men. They were holding the ship steady and on course. The man at the wheel nodded at me. The man at the compass waved bravely.

Rough water! I could
see a distant lighthouse on a
strong foundation of rock. I
was glad to see the light and
know we would be safe from
crashing into land.

    May 13. By sunup this
morning, the wind had died.
The sea became calm. Time to
get back to work. We checked
our nets and dropped anchor
near a school of silvery fish.

    As I leaned over the
rail, I saw a strange sight.

9

Suddenly, a small brown spider crawled across the page. Flora jumped and tossed the journal into the air. Glen caught it before it hit the floor.

"Don't be silly," said Glen. "That was just a little thing. What are you afraid of?"

"I'm not afraid, just startled," said Flora with a frown. "Now you read a little bit so we can find out what Salty Jones saw in the water."

Glen took the journal from Flora. The spider crawled into a crack in the floor.

I couldn't tell what was there at first. The surface of the water looked as white as snow or ice. Yet I knew there were no icebergs drifting this far south.

Then a spout of water twenty feet tall shot up from the ocean's surface.

"It's a whale!" I said to my mate. "It's a white one at that!"

The whale slowly circled our ship. At one point I could see its eye. At another point I could see its fin and then its huge tail. It seemed to be watching us carefully.

One of my crew shouted, "A white whale is good luck. It can lead you to great treasures!"

I had heard the stories before. My men and I quickly pulled the nets from the water. If we found treasure, we would never have to fish again!

Suddenly, the white whale lifted its tail and slapped the water with a mighty blow. It dove into the depths and disappeared.

"We must follow it!" I said.

"I never knew there was such a thing as a white whale," said Flora.

"I wonder if the legend is true," said Glen. "Maybe they followed the white whale and found a treasure."

"What if the whale led them to a secret island?" said Flora, taking the log back from Glen. "I bet there were lost pirate chests buried in the sand, full of gold and silver!"

"And rubies and diamonds and pearls!" said Glen. "I bet they got so rich they never had to go fishing again!"

May 15. We have been looking for the white whale for several days. We have not seen it again, but won't give up. We have talked about what we will do with our riches when we find them. My mate will buy his own ship. I will build a big mansion for my family.

May 20. It has been a week and there is no sign of the whale yet. My mate thinks we should give up but I am not ready. I know the whale is out there. We fished today so we would have something to eat. But we keep on hunting and hoping.

May 29. Today I told my men that I knew the search must end. We cannot chase a dream and starve while we do it. This morning we changed our course to head back home. We will fish as we go. Some we will eat and the rest we will sell when we reach the harbor. I won't make enough money from the fish to build a mansion, but that is all right.

June 15. We are home. Our fish are sold. Tonight I sleep in my own house. My family is glad I am back. In three days I will be off on the Sea Skipper to fish once more.

Flora closed the log. "Too bad Salty never found that white whale again," she said.

"Let's take this book to Grandpa and ask if he knows about the legend," said Glen.

"Yes," said Flora. "And Grandpa has a fishing boat. Maybe he will take us out in it. We can look for the white whale ourselves!"

They hurried to the attic door. "If we find a white whale," said Flora, "maybe we can follow him to the treasure!"

Glen smiled. "We did find something fun up in this old attic after all!"